WITCH'S BROOM

by RUTH CHEW

Illustrated by the author

SCHOLASTIC BOOK SERVICES

NEW YORK • TORONTO • LONDON • AUCKLAND • SYDNEY • TOKYO

ISBN: 0-590-72124-0

Copyright © 1977 by Ruth Chew. All rights reserved. This edition is published by Scholastic Book Services, a division of Scholastic Magazines, Inc., by arrangement with Dodd, Mead & Company.

12 11 10 9 8 7 6 5 4 3 2 1   2   1 2 3 4 5/8
Commonwealth Edition   11
Printed in the U.S.A.

WITCH'S
BROOM

Books by Ruth Chew published in
paperback by Scholastic Book Services

To Elsa Dunbar

1

CRASH!

"Amy! Why must you always run in the house?" Mrs. Perkins bent down to pick up her button box. Buttons were rolling all over the dining-room floor.

"I'm sorry, Mother." Amy got down on her hands and knees to pick up the buttons.

"See if you can find a button to match your blue skirt," her mother said.

Amy picked up all the blue buttons she could see and gave them to her mother.

Mrs. Perkins sat at the dining-room table and held each button in turn against Amy's skirt. "Why don't you sweep up the rest of the buttons, Amy? You can try out the broom I found in the back yard today."

"In the back yard?" Amy stood up. "Someone must have thrown it over the fence."

"That's what I thought," her mother told her. "I asked all the neighbours. Nobody knew where the broom came from. So I kept it. We need a new one anyway. Our old broom looks like something only a witch would want."

"Where did you put the one you found?" Amy asked.

"It's in the laundry room, next to the old broom." Mrs. Perkins picked up a button, looked at it, and put it down again.

Amy raced through the kitchen and down the basement stairs to the laundry room. In the corner by the washing machine were a dustpan and one scraggly broom. Amy was sure it was the old broom. She looked all around the laundry room. But this was the only broom she could find. She went back upstairs.

"I couldn't find the new broom," Amy told her mother. "You must have put it somewhere else."

"Maybe I did," Mrs. Perkins said. "Use the old one. It's better than nothing."

Amy went down to the laundry room again. She stared at the corner by the washing machine. Now she saw two brooms there!

How could she have missed it? It was such a pretty little broom, with a brown wooden handle and bright blue bristles. Amy picked up the dustpan and the little blue broom. She took them upstairs and began to sweep.

"I see you found the new broom." Mrs. Perkins went on looking for a button to match Amy's skirt.

Amy swept and swept. There always seemed to be more buttons on the floor.

"Aren't you finished yet, Amy?" Her mother stood up and took the little broom. She swept it three times across the floor. "There's something caught in it."

"It's a button." Amy bent over and tried to pick it out. The bristles seemed to keep snapping back over the button.

Her mother turned the broom upside-down. She grabbed the button with her thumb and forefinger and pulled it out. "Look at this, Amy!"

Mrs. Perkins held the button up to the light. It sparkled like a jewel. "Do you think it's too fancy, Amy?"

"It's beautiful!" Amy said.

Her mother smiled. "This is a magic broom," she said. "It found just the right button for you. I'd better sew it on before it gets lost." She handed the broom to Amy and went to get a needle and thread.

Amy set to work to sweep up the rest of the buttons. But now the blue bristles seemed to be all soft and limp. Amy couldn't get the broom to work at all. At last she carried it back to the laundry room and put it in the corner by the washing machine. She took the old broom up to the dining room to finish the job.

2

Amy's mother and father had both gone to work. It was summer time. Amy didn't have to go to school. She sat and looked out of the kitchen window.

It was nice to have a garden in the middle of Brooklyn. Amy watched a family of starlings splashing in the birdbath.

The doorbell rang. Amy ran to answer it. Her friend Jean Remsen stood on the door step.

"Come in, Jean," Amy said. "I was just watching the birds take a bath."

Jean followed Amy through the house and out into the yard. As soon as the back door opened, all the starlings in the birdbath flew up into the apple tree. They sat there, shaking their wings to dry them.

Jean walked over to the bird feeder in the peach tree near the back fence. "It's empty."

"There's some birdseed in the laundry room," Amy told her.

The birdseed was on top of the clothes dryer in a large plastic bag. Jean helped Amy carry it up the basement stairs and out the back door.

Neither of the girls was tall enough to reach the bird feeder. Amy went to get the kitchen stepstool. Jean climbed up on it and took the roof off the bird feeder.

There was a scoop in the bag with the

birdseed. Amy handed Jean a scoopful of seed to fill the feeder.

A little brown sparrow was sitting on a high branch on the peach tree. When he saw what Jean was doing he let out a high-pitched whistle. Amy heard another whistle, farther off. Then another. Before Jean had finished filling the feeder, the peach tree was crowded with little birds.

Jean climbed down and picked up the stepstool. At once the bird feeder was covered with fluttering sparrows. Birdseed sprayed out into the air around the feeder. It fell to the ground where some of the birds picked it up.

Amy was carrying the bag of birdseed. At the back door she turned to look at the birds. "My mother calls them flying pigs," she said. "They eat so much."

Jean took the stepstool into the kitchen. She came back to help Amy carry the heavy bag of birdseed down to the laundry room. "There must be a hole in the bag," Jean said. "It's leaking."

Amy looked. Birdseed was pouring all over the steps. "Hold your hand over the hole, Jean." She ran to the kitchen and came back with a big green trash bag.

The girls put the birdseed bag into the trash bag. Then they carried it down to the laundry room and put it back on the clothes dryer.

"It won't take long to clean up the spilled seed," Amy said. "We have two brooms." She picked up the dustpan from the corner.

Jean took a broom. It was the old one. Amy looked for the new broom. She couldn't see it anywhere. She had put it right there by the washing machine. But it was gone!

3

T<small>HAT</small>'s funny," Amy said.

"What is?" Jean asked.

Amy told her about the new broom.

"Your mother moved it," Jean said.

The girls searched all over the house, upstairs, downstairs, and in the basement. At last Amy caught sight of something blue behind the furnace.

It was the little broom, standing among the garden tools. The blue bristles were almost hidden by a spade. The brown handle was the same as those of the fork and the rake. If the spade had been a little wider, Amy wouldn't have been able to find the broom.

Amy was sure her mother would never have put the broom among the dirty tools. "It's just as if it's hiding from us," she told Jean.

"Don't be silly, Amy." Jean picked up the new broom.

The two girls went to work to clean the back stairs. Every time they thought they had swept up the seed, they found more. At last Jean put down the blue broom. "I give up."

Amy swept up the rest of the seeds with the old broom. Then she picked up the blue broom to put it away. "Jean!" Amy whispered. "The broom is *shaking*! I think it's laughing at us."

"Oh, stop your fooling, Amy." Jean grabbed the blue broom. "Let's go look at the birds."

4

Amy and Jean were looking out of the kitchen window. The sparrows were still fighting for first place at the feeder. A pair of graceful mourning doves pecked away at the seed on the ground.

"Oh, look! Isn't that bird pretty!" Jean pointed to a little brown bird with a rosy chest and a rosy patch on its back.

"That's a purple finch," Amy told her. "We only have one pair that comes to the feeder."

Suddenly a beautiful bird with blue wings and a crested head swooped down. It landed on the tree.

"That's the best-looking bird yet," Jean said. "It's bigger than the sparrows but not as big as the doves."

"That's a bluejay," Amy said. "Mother doesn't like them. She always chases them away. They have a cry that sounds like *Thief! Thief!* Mother says they're the ones who are the thieves. She says other birds are afraid of them. The bluejays steal their eggs. I don't believe it. They're so beautiful I can't help liking them."

"I think your mother is right," Jean said. "My mum says beauty is as beauty does. I'm going to drive that bird away." Jean was still holding the blue broom. She rushed out onto the yard and waved the broom at the jay.

"Thief! Thief!" the jay screamed. It flew straight at Jean.

The back door was open. Amy was standing in the doorway. She just had time to jump out of the way before Jean came rushing through into the kitchen. The bluejay was close behind her.

Amy slammed the door shut to keep the bird from flying into the house. She turned to Jean. "Why did you come in here in such a hurry? Don't tell me you're afraid of a bird!"

Jean was stretched out on her stomach on the kitchen floor. She was holding onto the broom with both hands. For a minute she didn't say a word.

Then Jean stood up. "Come and get your broom, Amy," she whispered. "You're right. There *is* something funny about it. It *pulled* me into the house!"

5

WHAT do you mean?" Amy stared at the broom.

Jean held onto the back of a kitchen chair to steady herself. "The broom flew back into the house. I was holding it and I got dragged along."

"Mother was right," Amy said. "She told me it was a magic broom. But she was only joking. She didn't know it could fly." She thought for a moment. "I wonder if we could ride on it."

"You go first," Jean said.

"I don't think it likes me. I can't even get it to sweep." Amy picked up the broom.

"Maybe it just doesn't like sweeping," Jean said.

Amy straddled the broomstick. "Come on, Blue Boy, let's go for a ride."

The broom seemed to quiver. Suddenly it began to jog around the kitchen. The blue bristles dragged on the floor. So did Amy's feet.

"Ow!" Amy's ankle banged against one of the kitchen chairs. She held tight to the broomstick and tried to yank it upright. "Up, Blue Boy, up!"

Without any warning the broom zoomed up into the air. Amy ducked her head just in time to keep it from crashing into the ceiling. "Steady, Blue Boy, steady!"

The broom bounced up and down. It seemed to be trying to throw Amy to the

ground. She wrapped her legs around the stick and hung on with both hands. "Easy, Boy, easy!"

Jean started to laugh. "You look like a cowboy on a bucking bronco."

"Maybe you think you can do better," Amy snapped.

At this the broom glided to the floor. Amy got off. She handed the broom to Jean. "Your turn."

Jean stroked the broom handle. "Nice Blue Boy," she said. She patted the blue bristles. Then she sat down on the bristles and waited. The broom lay quiet on the floor. "Please, Magic Broom," Jean said, "won't you take me for a ride?"

Still the broom lay on the floor.

All at once Amy had an idea. "Maybe it's a *girl!*"

Jean stood up. She turned the broom over and held it with the bristles up.

"What a pretty broom it is! Of course it's a girl."

Very slowly the broom swayed back and forth.

"Look, Jean," Amy said. "She's trying to nod. And I think she likes to have her bristles up."

Again the little broom nodded.

"No wonder she was angry with me," Amy said. "I was holding her upside-down!"

6

IF she's a girl, we can't call her *Blue Boy*," Jean said. "And *Blue Girl* sounds awful."

Amy was running her fingers through the blue bristles. "What about *Wispy*? Would you like to be called *Wispy*, pretty broom?"

The broom stood still, as if she were thinking. Then she swayed back and forth. Amy gave the bristles a little hug.

The broom did a tap dance on the floor with the end of her broomstick. She flew, bristles up, once around the room. Then she glided down in front of Jean and Amy and floated, with her stick level, about two feet above the floor.

"You mean you *want* to take us for a ride now, Wispy?" Amy asked.

The broom tipped back and forth as if to nod. The whole broom leaned forward, not just the bristles. It wasn't exactly like a nod; but Amy and Jean knew what it meant.

"Can you carry both of us?" Jean wanted to know.

The broom nodded again.

Amy sat down on the broom, facing the bristles. She held onto the broomstick with both hands. Jean sat behind her and put her arms around Amy's waist.

"Okay, Wispy," Amy said. The broom rose in the air. She flew out of the kitchen

into the dining room. Then she circled round and round the living room. She flew up the stairs, down the upstairs hall, and in and out of all the bedrooms.

The broom went up and down and round and round the house. At last she flew into Amy's room and landed on the bed. Amy and Jean got off.

The little broom still lay on the bed.

"I think she's tired, Amy," Jean said.

Amy pulled the covers over the broomstick. She tucked the pillow under the blue bristles. Then she closed the venetian blinds. The two girls tiptoed out of the room and closed the door.

7

Jean looked at the kitchen clock. "I'd better go home for lunch."

"Let's have a picnic," Amy said.

"I'll go ask Mum," Jean said.

Amy let Jean out of the front door and then went back to the kitchen. She looked through the window. The bluejay was still sitting on a low branch of the peach tree. The sparrows were all over the bird feeder.

That's funny, Amy thought. Sparrows are usually afraid of bluejays.

Amy watched the birds until the doorbell rang. Jean had come back.

"Mum said it was okay for me to eat lunch with you." Jean handed Amy a paper bag. "She gave me these for us to have for dessert."

Amy peeked into the bag. "Yum, doughnuts!"

The two girls made peanut butter and jelly sandwiches. They pulled two bananas from the bunch on the kitchen table. Amy took paper cups from the kitchen dispenser and a container of milk out of the refrigerator. She found a folded piece of red and white checked oilcloth in the bottom drawer of the sink cabinet. Then the girls went out into the yard.

Jean sat in the swing under the apple tree. Amy unfolded the oilcloth on the flagstone path and used it as a tablecloth. When the picnic was all spread out, Amy set up a garden chair for herself. "May I offer you a sandwich, Jean?"

"Thank you." Jean took one.

All at once a bright streak of blue flew down from the peach tree and landed on the checked tablecloth. It was the jay.

"Look at the dainty lady who wants to join our picnic!" Amy said.

Jean edged the swing back from the tablecloth. "It's that nasty bird. Amy, chase it away."

Amy looked at the beautiful bird. The

jay tipped her head with the cocky crest.
She reached out a claw. Amy broke off the
corner of her sandwich and gave it to the
bird. The bluejay nodded and chirped
something. Then she stood on one foot
while she held the piece of sandwich with
the other. She pecked away at the bit of
bread. When she finished it, she wiped her
mouth with the back of her claw.

Amy took a bite of her sandwich. Jean was too busy watching the bird to eat. When Amy finished the sandwich she poured a little milk into a paper cup and offered it to the bird. The bluejay put her beak to the edge of the cup. She didn't lift her head high in the air to swallow, as Jean had seen other birds do. Instead she waited for Amy to tip the cup. Then she drank.

Jean kept on watching the bird.

"Aren't you going to eat your lunch, Jean?" Amy asked.

Jean began to nibble her sandwich. But she kept her eyes on the bird.

The bluejay was walking around the tablecloth. When she came near the swing, Jean stood up and moved away.

Amy peeled a banana and handed a chunk of it to the bluejay. At dessert time the jay seemed to enjoy the doughnuts just as much as Jean and Amy did. She hopped over to her paper cup. Amy helped her take a drink.

While they were having lunch a dark cloud had come over the sun. A few raindrops splashed on the flagstones.

Jean helped Amy gather up all the picnic things. She whispered in Amy's ear, "Whatever you do, don't let that bird into the house!"

Amy thought for a minute. Then she handed Jean the paper bag, the cups, the milk container, and the banana peel. All Amy carried was the oilcloth.

It was raining harder now. The bluejay sat on a branch of the peach tree and watched the girls. When Jean opened the back door, the bird flew down.

Amy was ready. She waved the tablecloth in the air and swished the bird away from the door. Then she ducked in after Jean and slammed the door shut behind her.

8

"Whew!" Amy flopped down on a kitchen chair. She looked at Jean with admiration. "How did you know the bird wanted to get into the house?"

Jean was busy putting the picnic trash into the waste basket and the banana peel into the dustbin. She took the oilcloth from Amy and wiped it on both sides with a wet paper towel. Then she folded it and gave it to Amy to put away.

"Well?" Amy said. "What about the bluejay?"

"Don't you remember that the bird was trying to get in once before?" Jean said. "That was when Wispy pulled me into the house."

Amy frowned. "I wonder why Wispy did that."

"She must be afraid of the bluejay," Jean said. "There's something spooky about that bird."

Amy put the milk container into the refrigerator. "You're as bad as my mother about bluejays, Jean. This is the tamest bird I ever saw. Maybe she got away from a circus. And maybe she isn't used to living outdoors. That could be why she wants to come into the house." Amy peeked out of the kitchen window. The bluejay was sitting on a branch of the peach tree. "Wouldn't it be fun to have a bird like that for a pet?"

Bang! Amy looked up at the ceiling.

Her bedroom was right over the kitchen.

"Your pet broom must have fallen out of bed," Jean said.

The two girls ran out of the kitchen and up the stairs. When they opened the door of Amy's room, they saw the broom flying round and round. She was crashing into the furniture and banging against the walls.

"Take it easy, Wispy," Amy said. "We didn't mean to lock you in."

The broom slowed to a stop and floated just above the heads of the two girls.

"Since you want so much to get out, Wispy," Amy said, "what about taking us to the park?"

"It's raining," Jean reminded her.

"We could take an umbrella," Amy said. "I like the park in the rain. It's not crowded."

The broom flew to the window. She

poked her blue bristles between the slats of the venetian blind. Amy pulled up the blind. The rain was rattling against the windowpane.

All at once something crashed against the glass.

"It's the bluejay!" Jean said. "She's still trying to get into the house."

The bird was hovering just outside the window. She looked straight at the little broom.

Wispy backed away from the window. She wagged back and forth.

"You mean you don't want to take us to the park?" Jean sat down on the bed.

The broom nodded.

Jean looked at Amy. "Your broom doesn't like to sweep. Now she doesn't want to fly. What is she good for?"

The blue bristles drooped.

"*Sh-sh.*" Amy lowered the blind. She

patted the little broom. Suddenly she had an idea. "I'll bet I know what she'd like to do. Wispy, how about a game of Hide and Seek?"

The broom seemed to be thinking. For a minute she didn't move. Then she gave a little jump in the air. All the bristles perked up.

"Do you know the rules?" Jean asked.

The broom wagged, "No."

Jean explained the rules of the game. "No cheating, Wispy!" she said. "Amy, how will we know if Wispy is peeking when we hide?"

Amy thought for a minute. "We'll use the living room sofa as home base," she said. "Wispy has to keep her bristles under a sofa pillow while she's counting. And she has to tap out her counts with the end of her stick."

"What about 'Ready or not, here I come'?" Jean asked.

"Wispy can bang that out in rhythm, like this." Amy tapped with her foot to show what she meant.

"And if she finds one of us and gets to the sofa first, the one who's caught has to admit it," Jean said. "You can be It first, Amy."

They played Hide and Seek all over the house. Wispy was skinnier than Amy or Jean. It was easier for her to hide. But the girls knew all the best hiding places.

The broom seemed to think that Amy and Jean were small enough to hide in a drawer. She poked her bristles into any drawer that was open even a little bit. And she kept looking in the closets.

One time Amy found the broom behind the ironing board in the corner of

the kitchen. Wispy caught Amy hiding under her mother's bathrobe. It was hanging on the back of a chair. Twice Jean hid in a place where neither Wispy nor Amy could find her.

Amy had just counted to eighty-seven when the front door opened. Her father came into the house. "Is your mother

home yet, Amy?" he wanted to know.

Amy lifted her head from the corner of the sofa. "What time is it, Daddy?"

"A quarter to six," Mr. Perkins told her, looking at his watch.

Jean crawled out from behind the sofa. "I'd better rush," she said. "I'm late for supper already. See you tomorrow, Amy."

9

Amy, what in the world is the new broom doing in the stall shower?" Mrs. Perkins asked.

"Oh, is that where she's hiding?" Amy said. She was getting undressed to go to bed. "Jean and I were playing a game with her."

Mrs. Perkins came into Amy's room. She handed Amy the little blue broom. "Take it down to the laundry room and put it away. I'm going to take a shower. Or do you think the broom wants to take one first?" Amy's mother laughed and went back to the bathroom.

Amy felt the broom shudder. "What's the matter, Wispy?" She patted the blue bristles. "You're not afraid of my mother, are you?"

The broom stayed still while Amy carried her downstairs. There was a large box of rags in the laundry room. Amy put Wispy to bed there. Then she went back upstairs.

After her bath Amy went to bed and fell asleep. Sometime later in the night she woke. Light was coming through the slats in the venetian blind and streaming across her pillow.

She slipped out of bed and ran to the window to pull up the blind. It had stopped raining, and all the clouds had blown away. A full moon had risen over the houses behind the back yard. It was the moonlight that had wakened Amy.

There were still a few lights on in the houses. And Amy could hear the sounds of Brooklyn traffic. But all the birds had gone to sleep. A breeze rustled the leaves of the peach tree.

Something brushed against her shoulder. Amy turned to see the broom floating in the air beside her.

Amy looked out of the window again. "It's a lovely night for a ride," she whispered.

There was just enough moonlight in the shadowy room for Amy to see the broom nod.

10

Amy pushed up the window screen. She climbed onto the sill. Wispy moved closer to her. Amy sat down on the broom, facing the blue bristles. She held tight to the stick. Without a sound the little blue broom flew out of the window.

She soared over the peach tree. Then she flew higher and sailed over the roofs of the houses.

Amy looked down. Far below she could see the lights of Ocean Parkway. The broom was so high now that it made Amy dizzy. She closed her eyes.

When she opened them the moon seemed even brighter than before. There were no lights from the city now. They were flying over a dark forest. Deep inside her Amy had a funny feeling. Where was the broom taking her? She had to keep telling herself that she was not afraid.

In the bright moonlight Amy saw that the ground below was getting hilly. As they flew along the hills were taller. Amy noticed that the tops of some of the hills had no trees growing on them. They were sharp and rocky. They must be mountains.

Wispy headed for the highest mountain of all. She flew down. It seemed as if they were going to crash into the rocks.

Amy opened her mouth to scream. But instead of crashing into the mountain the little broom flew into the open mouth of a dark cave. It was blacker in here than anything Amy could remember. She couldn't even see the broom she was riding on.

It was cold in the cave. Amy wished she had a bathrobe over her thin summer nightgown.

For a while they flew on in the darkness. Then, far ahead, Amy saw a dim light. Wispy seemed to be slowing down. Amy could see the shape of the broom now. Soon she made out the rocky walls of the tunnel they were flying through. Wispy flew slower and slower. She stayed close to one side of the tunnel and kept stopping as if to look at what was ahead.

The light was getting brighter. It had a red glow. Now the air was warmer. The tunnel was coming to an end. Ahead of them was a very big cave.

The blue broom landed on a rocky ledge. Amy got off. The ledge ran all around the cave. It was high up near the ceiling and was all in shadow.

The light came from a huge fire that

blazed in the center of the cave. Around the fire was a crowd of people. Some were dressed all in red. Some in white. Some in black. And they all had brooms to match. One or two were sitting on their brooms.

Unlike the way Amy sat on Wispy, they sat on the bristles of their brooms, with the sticks pointing up in the air. They all wore hats. And the hats pointed up in the air too.

Amy was in a den of witches!

II

In the very center of the cave was a large flat rock. The fire had been built on the rock. A big iron pot steamed away on the fire. One of the witches was stirring the pot with a long-handled spoon.

Amy saw that this was the only witch who was wearing purple. She was tall and thin and looked very old. The witch was throwing things into the pot and chanting something in a cracked high-pitched voice.

The other witches were talking among themselves. A green witch showed the others what she had in a green bag. Some of them reached into the bag and brought out little squirmy things. Each one gave the green witch something in return. Sometimes there seemed to be an argument going on. The voices became louder. Amy heard someone scream, "Four mother-of-pearl buttons is too much to ask for a lizard. Three is more than enough!"

The old witch in the middle stopped chanting. She banged three times with her spoon on the rim of the iron pot. It sounded like a gong, echoing back from the sides of the dark cave.

All the witches stopped talking. They turned to face the purple witch. She pulled a scroll of paper from the pocket of her baggy skirt. "Roll call!" she said in a raspy voice.

Then she began to read a list of names.

"Abigail, Adelaide, Alice, Audrey." As each name was called, a witch waved her broom in the air and cried, "Here!"

"Barbara, Betsy, Bertha, Beryl." The old witch stopped. "BERYL!" she repeated. "Don't tell me that silly blue witch has skipped the meeting again!" The purple witch looked around the cave. She frowned. "Beryl!" she yelled. "I'll have no more of your nonsense. If you don't answer me, I'll have to ask you to

turn in your hat and your broom!"

Amy could see that the little broom was getting very excited. She banged against Amy and seemed to be trying to tell her something. Then she flew down near the witches. She stayed just behind them and reared up in the air to wave herself back and forth.

Amy took a deep breath and shouted at the top of her voice. "Here!"

The old witch nodded. She almost

seemed to smile. "There. That's better." She went on calling the roll. "Caroline, Catherine, Colleen."

Amy felt something nudge her. Wispy was back. She was hovering in the air beside Amy. Her bristles were twitching, and she kept giving little jumps. Amy climbed onto the broom. She stroked the blue bristles to calm them.

The little broom flew silently through the shadows out of the big cave and into the dark tunnel. Then faster and faster she went.

Amy wondered who Beryl was. Why did Wispy care if she lost her hat and her broom?

The cold air whistled past. Amy shivered in her thin nightgown. But she held tight to the broomstick and only wished the broom could fly faster.

12

Next morning was Saturday. Amy's mother and father didn't have to go to work. They slept late. So did Amy. She was wakened by the sound of the doorbell.

Amy jumped out of bed and ran downstairs to the front door. "Hi, Jean. Come on in. I just woke up. Mother and Dad aren't up yet. Would you like to wait in the yard for me? I'll be dressed in a minute."

Amy ran back upstairs. When she came

down again she went out into the back yard.

Jean was sitting in the swing, watching the birds. The bluejay was on the rim of the birdbath. She was standing on one foot and trying to wash her face with the other. A sparrow flew into the birdbath and began to splash around in the water. The bluejay drew back as if she didn't want to get anything more than her face wet. The sparrow went on splashing. Finally the jay flew away.

"That sparrow certainly isn't worried about bluejays," Jean said.

A big black-and-white tomcat squeezed through the picket fence from the neighbours' yard. The sparrow at once fluttered up into the peach tree.

"Hello, Domino." Amy stooped to pet the cat.

"You wasted half the day in bed," Jean

said. "I wanted to go somewhere on the broom."

"I already went somewhere," Amy told her. "That's why I slept so late."

"You mean you were out last night? What did your mother say?" Jean asked.

"Sh-sh! My mother doesn't know. And I don't want her to find out. She didn't much like it when she found Wispy in my bed."

The girls were in the back of the yard. Jean sat in the swing, and Amy stood behind her. Jean couldn't wait to hear about Amy's trip on the broom. "Tell me all about it. Where did you go?"

"I don't really know where I went," Amy said. She told Jean the whole story of her adventure with the witches.

The bluejay sat on the picket fence with her head cocked to one side.

"Are you sure you didn't dream the

whole thing?" Jean said when Amy had finished.

Amy looked around at the sunny yard. The black-and-white cat rubbed against her leg. Bees hummed in the roses on the bushes near the fence.

"How could I be so silly?" Amy laughed. "It must have been a dream." She gave the swing a push and sent Jean flying up into the air.

Mrs. Perkins opened the back door. She was holding the little blue broom. "Amy, must you leave this broom all over the house? I just found it in the spare room."

Amy knew she hadn't left the broom there, but she couldn't tell her mother.

Mrs. Perkins caught sight of the blue-jay. She ran over to the fence and waved the broom at the bird. Amy thought the bird would get hurt. But the bristles seemed to bend away from the bluejay. The bird flew up into the peach tree.

"Don't chase her, Mother," Amy said. "She's a tame bird."

"Bluejays are nasty," her mother said. "Come into the house now and have your breakfast. Maybe Jean would like something too. What do you girls want to eat?"

Amy let go of the swing. It coasted to a stop. Jean got off. "Thank you, Mrs. Perkins," she said, "but I've had breakfast."

"What are you doing with the new broom, Mother?" Amy asked.

"I was just going to use it to sweep the front path. I wish children wouldn't throw down bubble-gum wrappers." Mrs. Perkins went into the house.

Amy chased after her. "Use the old broom, Mother, please," she begged. "You'll get the new one all dirty."

13

Wʜɪʟᴇ Mrs. Perkins was sweeping the front path with the old broom, Amy was eating breakfast in the kitchen. Jean sat and watched her eat. The little blue broom leaned against the table.

"You ought to train Wispy to come when you whistle," Jean said. "Then you wouldn't always have to look for her."

"What about it, Wispy?" Amy asked.

The broom nodded.

The girls heard the front door open. Mrs. Perkins had finished her sweeping and was coming back into the house.

"Quick, Wispy, go back to the laundry room," Amy said. "And when I whistle, come as fast as you can."

The broom flew down the basement stairs.

Amy's mother walked into the kitchen. "I have to clean the house. It will be easier for me if there's no one around. Why don't you two go for a picnic?"

"I'll have to ask Mum." Jean got up from the table and went through the house to the front door. "See you later, Amy," she called.

Jean lived right across the street. It wasn't long before she was back again. Mrs. Perkins was getting ready to make sandwiches.

"Mum says it's okay," Jean said. "She told me to try not to get my feet wet."

Mrs. Perkins laughed. "You fell in the lake last time you and Amy went to Prospect Park." She began to slice up the end

of a roast of beef. "Hand me the box of sandwich bags, please, Jean." She pointed to the kitchen cabinet. "It's on the second shelf, next to the jar of honey."

Amy found a string bag to pack the lunch in. It had handles that she could loop over her arm. She looked in the refrigerator. "Mother, may we take a couple of cans of cherry soda?"

"Just be sure you don't leave the can tops around." Mrs. Perkins went to the sink to wash four peaches.

When the lunch was ready, the girls packed it in the string bag. Amy ran up to her room to get a sweater. She tied it around her waist.

"What do you need that for?" Jean asked. "It's hot today."

Amy remembered how cold she had been in her dream last night. "We don't know where we're going," she said. "You'd better get a sweater too."

Jean ran home to get one. Amy waited until her mother went upstairs with a pail of water. Then she gave a whistle. She heard a crash. Wispy had knocked over a chair as she flew through the dining room.

Amy opened the front door. The broom flew out and floated over the door step. Jean was just coming up the steps, carrying her red sweater. She climbed up on the broom behind Amy.

Amy gave the blue bristles a pat. "Take us for a ride, Wispy."

14

Wispy took off at an angle and flew over the house across the street. Jean looked in an upstairs window. She saw her mother. Mrs. Remsen was smoothing the wrinkles out of the spread on Jean's bed.

A minute later the girls and the broom were high in the air. A little gust of wind struck them. Wispy changed direction. A seagull flew past. Wispy started to chase it across the sky.

Amy and Jean held tight to the broomstick. Jean leaned forward and put her mouth to Amy's ear. "Look! There's the bridge to Staten Island!"

Amy saw water and ships far below them. They were flying over the harbour.

The seagull swooped down toward the ships. The broom followed.

Suddenly the gull caught sight of something floating in the water. He pounced on it.

Splash!

Wispy was so close behind the gull that her bristles hit the water.

At once the broom reared up. She tried to fly skyward again. Instead she kept sinking lower.

Amy held onto the broomstick and leaned back to help the broom point at the sky. "Up, Wispy, up!"

The choppy waves of the harbour washed under them. Jean's feet dragged in the water. Amy held the string bag as

high as she could to keep it from getting wet.

The little broom struggled. She strained forward and rose from the water. Then she started to drop down again. All her bristles sagged.

Wispy made a great effort. She coasted over the front of a boat and landed on the deck between two iron poles.

Amy and Jean stood up. Amy picked up the broom. She handed the string bag to Jean.

The two girls looked around. An iron gate stretched across the front of the boat. A man, a woman, and a little boy were standing by the gate. The man was staring at Jean and Amy. He took off his glasses and polished them with his handkerchief. The woman put her hand to her forehead as if she had a headache. And the little boy was trying to hide behind his mother.

Amy looked into the boat. "Jean, there are cars in there."

"It's the ferry," Jean said.

The girls went up a stairway to the deck above. People were sitting on benches in a big cabin. Jean and Amy climbed another flight of stairs. On the top deck there was another cabin. Long benches faced the water on the outside deck. The girls found a seat on one of them.

A cool sea breeze blew across the deck. Amy and Jean put on their sweaters. They watched a tugboat pushing a big ocean liner up the channel. Two sailboats skimmed past the ferry. The sun glinted on the water.

"Isn't this great?" Amy said.

When the boat docked at Staten Island, the iron gates were opened, and the cars drove off the ferry. A ramp was lowered for people to walk ashore. Jean and Amy decided to stay on board.

"The ferry sails back to Manhattan from here," Amy said. "If Wispy can't fly, we can get a subway that will take us home."

"We don't have any money for the fare," Jean reminded her.

"Hand me the string bag, Jean," Amy said. "We might as well have lunch."

Jean gave her the bag. Amy opened it and handed Jean a peach. "This ought to make you feel better."

Amy looked at the blue broom. "Your bristles are soggy, Wispy." She remembered the way the broom had acted the day it rained and when her mother had talked about a shower. "Is that why you can't fly?"

The broom nodded.

"My feet are soggy," Jean said. "It doesn't keep me from walking."

The girls sat on the bench and ate their lunch. The wind tangled their hair.

The ferry sailed past the Statue of Liberty. It was headed for the tall buildings of Manhattan.

When they had drunk the last drop of cherry soda Jean and Amy went into the cabin to put their trash into a basket. Amy saw a sign saying *Women's Room Downstairs.* "Come on, Jean. I have an idea."

15

In the Women's Room Amy took a paper towel and started to rub the blue bristles. The woman who had the job of keeping the room clean came over to see what she was doing.

"That's not what those towels are put here for," the woman said.

"I know," Amy told her. "But if I don't dry these bristles, the broom can't fly. And we won't be able to go home."

For a moment the woman just looked at the two girls. Then she smiled. "In that case I suppose I'll have to let you have some towels." She pulled four paper towels from the dispenser and gave them to Amy. "Run along now, girls. I shouldn't be doing this."

Jean and Amy sat down in the big cabin to dry the bristles. They rubbed and rubbed. The paper towels were soaked through. But the bristles were still damp.

"We'd better not risk letting Wispy fly over water," Jean said.

The ferry had reached the shore. It nosed its way between two rows of wooden pilings. Now everybody had to get off the boat.

Amy and Jean walked through the iron gate into the terminal building. They went down the stairs and out into the street.

"Now, Wispy," Amy said, "do your best."

She let go of the broom. Wispy fell over onto her side and floated above the pavement. Amy and Jean sat down on her.

The broom began to fly forward. She hardly rose into the air at all. The girls' feet dragged on the pavement. The people who noticed them seemed to think they were riding on a strange sort of bicycle.

They followed the signs to the Brooklyn Bridge and flew over the walkway. The cables of the bridge crisscrossed on each side of them like a giant spiderweb.

When they reached the Brooklyn side of the East River, Wispy began to fly higher. Amy felt the bristles. "They're almost dry now," she told Jean.

"I wonder what time it is," Jean said. "My feet are soaking wet. I'd like to change my shoes."

Suddenly the little broom gave a bounce. She zoomed straight up in the air and took a short cut toward Amy's house. In almost no time they landed on the door step.

Amy stood up and picked up the broom. The front door opened. Mrs. Perkins looked out. "What are you doing with the new broom?" she asked.

"We were riding on it, Mother," Amy said.

Mrs. Perkins laughed. She took the empty string bag. "I see you fell in the lake again, Jean. The broom must have come in handy to pull you out."

"We couldn't have got home without it," Amy said.

16

At supper time Mrs. Perkins said, "There's a bluejay in the yard. I can't seem to drive her away."

Amy put down her fork. "Mother, that's the one I told you about. She's a tame bird. She wants to come into the house."

"When I was a boy," Mr. Perkins said, "I always wanted a parrot. Maybe we could make a pet of this jay."

"Nonsense." Amy's mother gave him a second helping of mashed potatoes. "Bluejays are not nice birds. And this one screams, 'Thief! Thief!' every time she sees me."

Amy's father laughed. "Maybe you have something that belongs to her." He got up from the supper table and went to look out of the dining-room window. It was still light outdoors. "There's the bird sitting on the fence. Isn't she beautiful?"

All at once Mr. Perkins dropped the table napkin he was holding. He ran into the kitchen and out the back door.

Amy and her mother got up from the table and followed him. When they went into the yard they saw Mr. Perkins standing beside the fence. He was holding the bluejay in his hands. "The neighbours' cat caught her," he said.

"Oh, the poor thing!" Mrs. Perkins turned her head away. "Is she dead?"

"I can feel her heart beating." Mr. Perkins stroked the blue feathers. "Let's take her into the house. She'll be safer there."

He carried the jay into the kitchen. Amy ran up to her room and brought down a shoe box. Mrs. Perkins lined the box with cotton and put the bird in it. "We'll let her rest for a while," she said. She put the shoe box on the kitchen table. The family went back into the dining room to finish supper.

After the meal they all carried their dishes out to the kitchen and put them into the dishwasher. While Amy's mother was scrubbing the frying pan, Amy and her father went to look at the bluejay.

"Her eyes are open," Mr. Perkins said. "I think she's feeling better."

Mrs. Perkins put down the frying pan and joined them. "Maybe she's hungry. Amy, you know where the birdseed is." She handed Amy an empty peanut butter jar. "You can put some in this."

Amy took the jar down to the laundry room. The blue broom met her at the foot of the stairs. She poked her bristles into the jar.

"I'm sorry, Wispy. I can't play with you, now," Amy said. "Be a good girl and don't get into any mischief." She went to fill the jar with birdseed from the bag on the clothes dryer.

Amy took the jar of birdseed up to the kitchen. Mr. Perkins tried to get the blue-jay to eat it. The bird looked at the seed and wouldn't open her beak.

"She's still in a state of shock," Mrs. Perkins said. "We ought to leave her alone for a while."

When her mother and father went into the living room to watch television, Amy went down to the laundry room.

"You must be tired, Wispy, after all the flying you did today." Amy felt the blue bristles. They were quite dry now. She put the broom into the box of rags and turned to go back upstairs.

Something rubbed against her shoulder. It was Wispy. She had hopped out of the box. Amy put her back again. "Go to sleep, Wispy."

Amy went back up the basement stairs. She turned around before she went into the kitchen. The little broom was gliding behind her.

"Wispy," Amy said. "I know you want to sleep in my bed, but my mother doesn't like it."

The blue bristles drooped. Amy carried the broom back down the stairs and once more put her in the box of rags. When she went back up to the kitchen she clicked the door to the basement stairs shut behind her.

Before she went to bed Amy peeked into the shoe box. The bluejay was fast asleep.

17

THE next day was Sunday. When Amy came downstairs in the morning Mr. Perkins was at the kitchen table making pancakes in the electric frying pan. Mrs. Perkins was measuring coffee into the coffeepot on the stove.

Amy looked into the shoe box. The bluejay was all huddled up in it. Her eyes were open, but she was quite still.

"Maybe she'll eat something now," Amy said.

The bluejay stood up in the box and stretched her wings. She looked across the table at the frying pan.

Mrs. Perkins had put the peanut butter jar of birdseed in the kitchen cabinet. She went to get it. The bird took one look at the seed and put her head under her wing.

"She's too frightened to eat. We'd better put her back outdoors." Mrs. Perkins picked up the shoe box and took it to the back door. When Amy's mother opened the door the bluejay flew up into the air. But instead of flying out into the yard she flew back into the kitchen. She perched on the back of one of the kitchen chairs.

Mr. Perkins laughed. "I think the bird wants to stay in the house."

"Of course she does." Amy poured herself a glass of orange juice. "I told you she's a tame bird."

Mr. Perkins put a pancake on Amy's plate.

The doorbell rang. Mrs. Perkins went

to answer it. "Come in, Jean. You're just in time to have some pancakes."

"Thank you, but I've already eaten four this morning," Jean told her.

"You'll never guess who spent the night at our house," Mrs. Perkins said.

Jean followed her to the kitchen. The bluejay was still perched on the back of the chair. Mr. Perkins had poured some birdseed into the palm of his hand. He offered it to the bird.

Jean stared. "I thought you said your mother hated bluejays, Amy."

"This jay was caught by the neighbours' cat yesterday," Mrs. Perkins said. "We brought her into the house to keep her safe. And now she doesn't want to leave."

"We can't get her to eat anything." Amy's father dumped the birdseed back into the peanut butter jar.

The bluejay watched him pour maple

syrup on his pancakes. She chirped at him. Then she flew up onto the moulding over the door.

Mrs. Perkins sat down at the table to eat her breakfast.

The bluejay was looking all around the room. The door of the kitchen cabinet was open a little. The jay walked quietly across the top of the door and then flew into the cabinet.

Jean had been watching the bird. "Amy," she said, "look where the bluejay is." She pointed.

Amy jumped up and ran to the cabinet. The jay was trying to get the top off the biscuit jar.

"Silly!" Amy said. "You can't eat biscuits first thing in the morning.

The bird fluttered up to the next shelf and began to poke her head into the cereal boxes.

Mrs. Perkins looked up. "Amy, get that bird out of there!"

Mr. Perkins walked over to the cabinet and reached up to grab the bluejay. She dodged him and knocked a box of corn-flakes onto the floor. Then she flew down to the kitchen table and peeked into the sugar bowl.

Mr. Perkins laughed. "I never saw such a nosy bird."

The bluejay squawked at him. Amy's

father laughed again and sat down to finish his breakfast.

Mrs. Perkins went down the basement stairs. She came back with the little blue broom.

The bluejay took her beak out of the sugar bowl. She gave one look at the broom and then stared straight at Amy's mother. "Thief! Thief!" she screamed.

Mrs. Perkins put the lid on the sugar bowl. "Thief yourself," she said. She began to sweep up the cornflakes.

Amy put the breakfast dishes into the dishwasher and wiped the crumbs from the table.

"I don't know what's the matter with this broom." Mrs. Perkins stopped sweeping. She frowned. "It doesn't sweep well at all."

"Let me finish sweeping the kitchen, Mother," Amy said. "There's a trick to using this broom."

18

Mr. and Mrs. Perkins went out of the kitchen. As soon as they had gone, Amy picked up the broom to carry it back to the laundry room.

"Watch out, Amy!" Jean ducked.

The bluejay flew over Jean's head and perched on the broom handle. She started to chatter at the broom. She seemed to be asking Wispy something. Wispy wagged "no." Then the bluejay looked at Amy and began to chatter again.

"She's trying to tell me something," Amy said.

The bird hopped off the broom and flew over to the toaster in the middle of the table.

"I wonder if she'd like some hot buttered toast." At once Amy felt the broom tip back and forth. She propped Wispy against the table and went to get a slice of bread to drop into the toaster.

The bird sat and waited for the toast to pop up. When it was ready Amy buttered the toast and cut it into small squares. The bluejay picked up each piece with her claws and nibbled it down to the last crumb.

"She acts as if she hadn't had anything to eat since our picnic the day before yesterday," Jean said.

While the bird was eating Amy and Jean heard a tapping noise. They looked at the broom. She was doing a happy little dance with the end of her broomstick on the floor.

"*Sh-sh*, Wispy! Suppose my mother and father come in here!" Amy picked up the little blue broom and carried her down to the laundry room. She came back with her mother's worn-out old broom and swept up the cornflakes. She propped the broom against the table while she went to get the dustpan.

The bluejay walked across the table to get a better look at the old broom. She tipped her head on one side. Then she hopped down onto the scraggly bristles. She sat there for a minute, like a bird on a nest.

"Look, Amy," Jean said, "the jay looks right at home on your old broom."

Suddenly the bird spread her blue wings and fluttered off the bristles. She flew out of the kitchen and through the dining room. Then she winged her way across the living room and up the stairs.

Mr. and Mrs. Perkins were sitting on the living room sofa reading the Sunday paper. When the bird flew through the room, Mrs. Perkins jumped to her feet. She chased after the jay.

Jean and Amy had followed the bird out of the kitchen. Now they ran upstairs to see what was going on.

The bluejay was flying in and out of all the bedrooms.

"She seems to be looking for something," Jean said.

The jay caught sight of a wastebasket. She flew down into it and started turning over all the rubbish.

Mrs. Perkins was holding a section of the newspaper. She put the paper over the top of the wastebasket like a lid. Then she picked up the basket. "This bird is quite well enough to go back outdoors." She took the wastebasket downstairs and went out onto the door step. First she closed the big glass front door behind her. Then she took the newspaper off the top of the wastebasket.

Amy's father had come to the door. Along with Jean and Amy he looked through the glass. They saw the bird fly out of the wastebasket. She flapped up into the sycamore tree in front of the house.

"Thief! Thief!" The bluejay screamed at Amy's mother.

Mr. Perkins opened the door for Mrs. Perkins to come in. "I'm sure we could have made a pet of that bird," he said.

"Wild birds belong outdoors," Mrs. Perkins said. She looked at Jean and Amy. "And so do children on a lovely day like this. Why don't you take the broom out and play horse with it? That's all it's good for."

19

Amy and Jean took the blue broom out on the door step. As soon as the door closed behind them Wispy tipped over on her side and floated in the air beside the girls.

They sat down, one behind the other, on the broom. Wispy sailed up into the air. But instead of flying across the street, she flew into the sycamore tree.

"Look, Jean," Amy said.

The bluejay was perched on a branch. Her feathers were fluffed out around her. She looked lonely and sad.

"I wish my mother would let her live in our house," Amy said. Then she told the broom, "Wispy, we can't stay here. My mother doesn't let me climb this tree."

The broom jiggled up and down. But she stayed in the tree. Suddenly there was a whirr of blue feathers. The jay landed on the bristles of the broom. At once Wispy flew out of the tree. She zoomed up over the houses.

The two girls held tight to the broomstick. They were going so fast that it almost took their breath away. For several minutes neither of them could say a word. Then Amy said, "You were wrong, Jean. Wispy doesn't seem to be afraid of the bluejay at all. I think she asked the bird to come along."

"Where are we going?" Jean wanted to know.

"Why don't we go to the beach?" Amy suggested.

"We didn't bring our bathing suits," Jean reminded her.

"We could go wading," Amy said.

Jean thought about this. "Wispy, take us to Coney Island."

The girls looked down. They were so high that they could see the ocean. But the broom was flying inland, away from the sea.

Amy tried to jerk the stick back. "Whoa!" she said.

Wispy kept right on flying the way she was going.

The bluejay was perched on the end of the bristles. She stared straight ahead. The wind whipped through her feathers.

"Maybe Wispy's afraid she'll get wet again," Jean said. "And that's why she won't go to the beach."

Amy was staring at the ground below. They were flying over a dark forest. "Jean," she said in a low voice, "it isn't

moonlight now. So I can't be sure. But that looks like the forest I saw in my dream."

"You mean the one about the witches?" Jean asked. "Wispy," she said to the broom, "turn around and go home now."

The broom didn't seem to hear her. She flew even faster. Now there were rolling hills below them. The hills became mountains. Far ahead Amy saw a tall bare mountain. The broom headed straight for it.

Now Amy was sure. "It wasn't a dream after all," she said.

20

THE bluejay cast a big black shadow on the mountainside. Then the little broom dived into the dark tunnel. The girls tried to hold onto each other and the broomstick at the same time. Very soon it was too dark for Jean to see Amy right in front of her. And it was cold.

Amy could tell that Jean was afraid, so she pretended to be very brave. But, deep inside, Amy was frightened too. Jean had been right all along. There *was* something spooky about the bluejay. And the broom was mixed up in the spookiness.

"We should have brought our sweaters," Amy said.

Jean's teeth were chattering. She looked into the blackness. It seemed an age before they saw a faint light.

"We must be coming to the big cave," Amy whispered.

This time Wispy didn't slow down. She kept flying at top speed. The light got brighter. The little broom sailed into the cave.

The fire on the flat rock was almost out. Only a little pale steam came from the big iron pot. The cave was much darker than before. At first Amy thought it was empty.

Then she caught sight of a pile of purple rags beside the big pot. Amy looked hard at it. Now she saw that it was the old witch. She was curled up on the rock, fast asleep. Her pointed purple hat had rolled off her straggly white hair. But she was still clutching her long-handled spoon.

Wispy headed for the flat rock. Before she reached it the bluejay fluttered off the broom. The bird flew to the witch and perched on her shoulder. She tickled the old woman's cheek with her blue wing.

The witch waved the spoon as if to brush the bird away. She let out a snore.

Again the bluejay tickled the old woman's cheek. This time the witch opened her green eyes. The bird flew off her shoulder.

At this moment the broom landed on the rock. Amy and Jean got off. Amy looked around for a place to hide. But it was too late.

The witch was wide awake now. She stared at the two girls. Then she looked at the broom. She put her hat back on her head and stood up. "Aren't you Beryl's broom? Where, may I ask, is Beryl?"

Amy and Jean stood as if they were frozen. The bluejay was circling round the rock. She flew down in front of the witch. The old woman bent over to take a good look at the bird. She straightened up and turned to Wispy. "Broom, something tells me this is Beryl. Am I right?"

The blue broom nodded.

"Too bad you can't talk, Broom," the witch said.

At this Wispy flew to Jean and Amy. The witch walked over to them. "And who are you?" she demanded in her harsh voice.

Amy's mouth felt dry. She swallowed. "This is Jean," she said, trying hard not to sound frightened. "And I'm Amy."

The witch took a long hard look at Amy. Then she bent over and picked up the bluejay. She stroked the bird's head with one bony finger. "Silly little witch," she said. "What did you do to get yourself in this condition?"

21

B<small>ERYL</small>," the old witch said, "tell me the truth! Did you lose the magic charm I gave you?"

The bluejay didn't answer. She hung her head and looked ashamed.

The witch turned to the broom. "You brought these girls here because you thought they could help. Didn't you?"

Wispy nodded.

The witch looked at Amy with her bright green eyes. "What do you know about all this?"

"Not very much," Amy said. "I knew Wispy was a magic broom, but I didn't know she belonged to a witch. And I thought the bluejay had escaped from a circus."

"A circus!" the witch rasped. "What do you mean?"

"She didn't really act like a bird," Amy said. "She held her food in her claws instead of pecking it off the ground. And she drank out of a cup."

The old witch frowned. "I can't understand how Beryl got into all this trouble so fast. She came to the meeting Friday night."

Before she had time to think, Amy said, "No, she didn't."

The witch grabbed her by the arm. "I thought you said you didn't know much about all this."

Amy looked into the witch's eyes. "I
don't. But I do know Beryl wasn't here
Friday night. I was the one who answered
when you called her name." Then Amy
told the old woman about her wild ride in

the middle of the night. "Next morning I thought it was just a dream," she finished.

"And how did you happen to have Beryl's broom?" the witch wanted to know.

"My mother found the broom under the peach tree in the back yard," Amy said. "And Jean discovered that the broom was magic when it pulled her into the house."

The old woman turned to look at Jean.

"I thought Wispy was afraid of the bluejay," Jean said. "But she must just have been trying to lead her into Amy's house. After that the bird was always trying to get in."

The witch was still holding the jay. She smoothed the blue feathers. "I suppose you know you're in an awful fix," she said to the bird.

"What do you mean?" Amy asked.

"She's changed herself into a bird and now she can't change back," the old woman told her.

"Why can't she? She's a witch, isn't she? Jean said.

"Beryl is only a beginner. She's not very good at magic yet." The old woman straightened her purple hat.

"Can't you help her?" Amy said. "You must be *very* good at magic."

The old woman cleared her throat. She looked pleased. "Well, yes, I am good at magic," she said, "quite good. But Beryl has lost the charm I gave her. You can't go losing charms, you know." She fiddled with the folds of her baggy skirt. "Oh, I suppose I might as well tell you. Only, mind you don't go blabbing it around." She lowered her voice. "Beryl is my granddaughter."

"Your granddaughter!" Amy and Jean said together.

"Yes, and I'm fond of her," the purple witch admitted. "But all the other witches would be very angry if they knew I gave her the strongest charm I have. It was a stupid thing to do. Beryl was always so silly. Fancy letting a broom fly bristles-forward just because it wants to!

"Now Beryl has used that powerful charm to change herself into a bluejay. She has lost the charm and can't change back. And none of my magic is strong enough to break the spell."

"Poor Beryl," Amy said. "What can we do to help?"

"Take her home with you." The old witch handed Amy the bluejay. "She doesn't like sleeping in trees. And once in a while let her have a little cake or ice cream. Beryl always did like strange things to eat. I never could get her to enjoy beetles' whiskers or any other proper witch food."

22

WHEN the broom flew out of the tunnel in the mountain there were dark clouds in the sky. The bluejay was perched on Amy's shoulder. It was more comfortable for her than the turned-up bristles of the broom.

Wispy was flying against the wind. The broom bounced up and down.

"Slow down, Wispy," Jean said. "My stomach can't stand this."

The broom flew faster.

"There's a storm coming," Amy said. "If Wispy's bristles get wet she won't be able to fly."

Far off there was the rumble of thunder.

Jean looked down. All she could see below were the tops of trees. She closed her eyes and tried not to feel the bouncing of the broom.

Amy was talking to the jay. "When we get home, Beryl," she said, "I'll have to hide you under my shirt to get you into the house. You can stay in my room."

Jean opened her eyes. A long fork of lightning streaked from one cloud to another. An instant later there was a crash of thunder. "Look!" Jean pointed to the forest below. A huge tree had split in two.

Amy felt a drop of water on her arm. Then another. The broom began to fly more slowly.

Jean was thinking hard. "Wispy," she

said, "if you flew with your bristles down I could sit on them. My dress would keep the rain off."

The broom stopped still in the air. The rain was splashing down. Wispy seemed to be thinking. Then she tipped up and down as if she were nodding.

"Hold still, Wispy," Jean said. "Amy's wearing jeans. We have to change places."

The jay flew off Amy's shoulder and fluttered over the broom. Jean grabbed Amy around the waist and swung around her. Amy slid along the broomstick. Jean landed on the bristles. She spread her dress over them.

Now Amy was facing Jean. If she didn't want to ride backward she had to turn around.

"Hurry, Amy," Jean said. "If Wispy points her stick up the bristles will be sure to stay covered. And I want to get home. My legs are getting scratched."

Amy felt like a high-wire performer in a
circus. She took a deep breath and swung
one leg over the broomstick. Now she was
sitting sideways. One more swing of her
legs and she was in front of Jean again.

The bluejay flew down to perch on the
end of the broomstick. She turned to look
at Amy. Then she clapped her wings.

Jean clapped too.

23

By the time the broom landed on Amy's door step the rain had stopped. Jean stood up and shook her dress. "You fly very well bristles-down, Wispy. Why don't you do it all the time?"

The blue broom wagged at her.

"I guess she still likes to fly her way." Amy picked up the broom. She put the bluejay under her shirt and tucked the shirt into her jeans.

"It must be past lunch time. I'd better go home." Jean crossed the street to her own house.

Amy rang the doorbell. Her mother opened the door. She reached for the broom. "I hope you don't mind if I use your horse to clean the cobwebs out of the boiler room."

Amy was sure Wispy wouldn't like it, but she had the bluejay under her shirt. She didn't want to argue with her mother.

Mrs. Perkins took a good look at Amy. "Goodness! You're soaking wet. Run up to your room and change. Then you'd better get something to eat. While you were out I baked a batch of brownies."

Amy felt the bird give an excited little flutter. She went into the house and ran upstairs. "Take it easy, Beryl," she whispered. "You'll get a brownie."

Amy went into her bedroom. She took the bluejay out from under her shirt and put her on top of the dresser. Then she opened a drawer to get a dry pair of jeans and a fresh shirt.

The bird hopped into the drawer. She

began to turn over everything in it.

"Don't mess up the stuff in there, Beryl." Amy slipped into the jeans and pulled the shirt over her head. "My mother likes me to keep the drawers neat."

Amy went down to the kitchen. Lunch was all ready for her on the table. She ate the cheese sandwich and the banana and saved the two fat brownies and the glass of milk for last.

Just as she was about to take her first bite of brownie, Amy remembered the

bluejay. She jumped up from the table and ran upstairs with the brownie.

Amy went to her bedroom, but the bluejay was no longer there. She looked in the bathroom and in the spare room. Beryl wasn't there. When Amy went into her parents' room she found the bird perched on top of her mother's dresser. The jay had opened the lid of the glass jewel box. She was picking Mrs. Perkins' earrings out of the box and dropping them on the floor.

"Beryl! Stop that!" Amy grabbed the bird and carried her to her own room.

She put the bluejay on her desk. "I brought you this." She placed the brownie beside the bird. "If you can't eat it all, save some for me. Mother only gave me two. And, Beryl, try to be good."

Amy went back to her parents' room. She picked up her mother's earrings and put them in the jewel box.

One of her father's dresser drawers was partly open. Mr. Perkins' handkerchiefs and socks were scattered around the room.

Amy folded the handkerchiefs and rolled the socks into neat little balls. She put them back into the drawer. When she went out of the room she clicked the door shut behind her.

Mrs. Perkins was in the kitchen. "Finish your milk, Amy," she said. "You must have liked the brownies. You didn't leave so much as a crumb."

24

Before she left for work next morning, Mrs. Perkins said, "You're too old to be going through the things in my room, Amy. I thought you'd grown out of that. I don't want to have to lock my door."

Amy didn't know what to say.

When her mother and father had gone she made the beds and put the breakfast dishes into the dishwasher. The doorbell rang. Amy went to answer it.

Jean stood on the front stoop. She was wearing dungarees. "Mum was pretty mad at me for getting wet two days in a row," she said. "My Sunday dress has to go to the cleaner."

"That reminds me." Amy pulled a pink slip of paper and a dollar bill out of her pocket. "Mother told me to pick up my skirt from the cleaner. Let's do it now before I forget."

"Where's Beryl?" Jean asked.

"I don't know," Amy said. "I haven't seen her this morning. That bird gets into everything. We'd better see what she's up to."

"Maybe she's with Wispy," Jean said.

The two girls went down to the laundry room. Wispy was leaning against the washing machine. The blue bristles were covered with spiderwebs. The jay was perched on one foot on the handle of Mrs. Perkins' scraggly old broom. Beryl was nibbling what was left of a brownie.

Amy glared at her. "Mother left that

for my lunch," she said. "I was going to
share it with you."

The bird chirped something. She swallowed the last crumb and flew up the
basement stairs.

Amy took a rag from the box. She used
it to wipe the spiderwebs from the little
broom.

The girls went to the cleaner on Church Avenue for Amy's skirt. It was in a big plastic bag.

"Look, Jean, this is the button I told you about." Amy felt the button through the plastic.

"The one Wispy found?" Jean asked.

Amy nodded. She hung the plastic bag over her arm, but she kept feeling the button.

On the way home they had to pass the bakery shop. Jean sniffed the air. She stopped to look at a gooey chocolate cake in the bakery window. "Wouldn't Beryl love to get her beak in that," she said.

"I'd like to see her *stuck* in it." Amy was still rubbing the button.

At that moment there was a shriek from the woman behind the counter in the bakery. Now Amy and Jean saw that a bird was flying round and round in the shop. The bird banged into the plate glass

window and fell, head-downward, into the
sticky chocolate icing on the cake. The
bird's feet stuck up in the air. Her blue
feathers were coated with chocolate, and
she couldn't fly.

"Amy!" Jean said. "That looks like
Beryl!"

The woman behind the counter was
yelling, "Somebody get it out of there."
But the other people in the shop just
crowded around to look at the bird. Amy
handed the skirt to Jean. She ran into the
bakery and pushed her way between the

people to grab the bird and pull her out of the cake.

"I'll wash the icing off her," Amy told the woman behind the counter. She took the bird out of the shop and started home. Jean came after her.

Once inside her house Amy went to the kitchen sink to rinse the bluejay. "Hang the skirt in my closet, Jean," she said.

When all the chocolate had been scrubbed from her feathers, Beryl hopped onto the drainboard. She stretched her wings and flapped them to get the water off. Then, without even a nod of thanks to Amy, she flew out of the kitchen.

Jean was just coming back into the room. She ducked as the bird whizzed past. "Where's Beryl going?"

"To find some more mischief, I guess." Amy dried her hands. "Come on out in the yard, Jean. Beryl doesn't want to be with us."

25

Amy stood on the swing and grabbed the chains. Jean sat on the seat and held onto Amy's legs. This way they could swing at the same time.

Jean was pumping hard to get the swing up in the air when both girls heard a sound from Amy's bedroom window. They looked up. Someone was pushing up the screen.

Amy couldn't believe her eyes. A small figure in a long blue dress and a pointed hat came flying out the window on a broom.

"It must be Beryl!" Jean whispered.

The little blue witch waved her hand at Amy and Jean. Then she tipped the broom handle back and flew high over the peach tree. The girls watched until she was only a blue speck in the sky. And then she was gone.

"What do you think happened, Amy?" Jean asked.

"I don't know anything except that Wispy is gone," Amy said.

Jean was afraid that Amy was going to cry. She changed the subject. "It's hot,

Amy. Let's get into our bathing suits."

When Amy's mother came home she found them splashing under the garden hose.

"Where's the broom, Amy?" Mrs. Perkins asked. "Your room needs sweeping."

"Isn't it in the laundry room?" Amy asked.

"No, there's only that silly little blue one you play with," her mother said. "Well, never mind. I'll use that."

Amy felt her heart jump. "Jean," she said. "No wonder Wispy didn't say goodbye. *She's still here!*"

Jean was thinking. "We should have known," she said slowly. "Beryl was riding a broom that flew with its bristles *down*."

Amy laughed. "Mother always said our old broom was just what a witch would want. Beryl must have enchanted it somehow."

Mrs. Perkins came out into the back yard. She was holding the little blue broom in one hand and Amy's blue skirt in the other.

"It's about time I bought a new broom," she said. "Take your pet, Amy." She handed Amy the broom. "Oh, and don't expect to wear this skirt for a while. Look. The cleaner lost the button."

Amy looked at the skirt. It was still in the plastic bag. Near where the button should have been, a raggedy little hole had been torn in the plastic.

"I think I'll just have to sew a plain white button on it." Mrs. Perkins took the skirt back into the house.

Amy stroked the little broom. Wispy rubbed against her shoulder.

"Now we know everything," Amy said.

"What do you mean?" Jean asked.

Amy grinned. "Beryl found her magic charm."